The Night of the Kelpies

by

Joan Lennon

Illustrated by Daniel Atanasov

To cats. Thank you!

First published in 2010 in Great Britain by
Barrington Stoke Ltd
18 Walker St, Edinburgh, EH3 7LP

www.barringtonstoke.co.uk

ISBN: 978-1-84299-758-1

Printed in Great Britain by Bell & Bain Ltd

Contents

Chapter 1
The House From Hell

"Well, this is it," said Maggie Grey. "This is your grandmother's house." Then she added in a whisper, "The house from hell."

Sandy Grey felt his heart sink. He and his mum had walked a long way. They'd left the main road and taken a bumpy dirt track that went all along the top of the cliffs. The sea smashed against the rocks below them. And in front of them was a dark, grim house.

Sandy didn't want to go in. It was stony and cold, and the windows were blank and empty.

They walked up to the door, but then his mum stopped. It was as if she was afraid to go in. Sandy looked at her. Her face was tight and worried.

We're a long way from our old life, thought Sandy. He'd hated saying good-bye to their flat and all his friends and everything he'd grown up with. Years ago, his father had gone away – vanished – from this very house. Since then, it had just been the two of them, which was OK. But then his mum lost her job, and now they couldn't afford city rents any more. Things looked bad, very bad ... and then they got a letter from his grandmother's doctor.

"She's had a fall," the letter said, "and broken her leg. She needs someone to come back here and look after her until it's better."

Sandy and his mum hadn't heard from the old woman in years. She didn't want to know them. And that was fine with Sandy's mum.

"Your dad and I lived with her when we were first married and it was *awful*. She was a mean old bag then – I don't know what she'll be like now! After all that's happened ... since your dad was lost ..." and then Sandy's mum stopped. She never talked much about Sandy's dad but she still kept a photo of him by her bed. His name had been Robert Grey.

When they got the doctor's letter, Sandy's mum wanted to say no, that they couldn't come and help. Sandy *really* didn't want to come. But in fact, looking after Sandy's grandmother was the answer to their problems. They had nowhere to live and Sandy's mum had no job.

Sandy took a deep breath. He walked up to the door.

"Right – let's do this!" he said. He pretended to pull two guns from his belt and blow the lock off the door. Then he pushed the door open. "Ladies first!" he whispered. "Most of all if it's dangerous!" His mum gave him a thin smile, and stepped in.

"Maggie? Is that you?" someone called out. It was a cold, mean voice with no welcome in it. The house smelled of damp and old age. They were standing in a dark corridor.

Sandy's mother gave a sigh, and then stood up straight.

"Yes, Mrs Grey, it's us," she called back.

Sandy stared at his mum. "Why do you call Dad's mother Mrs Grey?" he whispered as they went along the dark corridor towards a door at the end.

4

His mum didn't answer. She just pushed open the door.

The sitting room was cold, but the look on the old woman's face was even colder. She was sitting in a wheel-chair. One leg was in plaster and stuck out in front of her.

"There's some food in the kitchen you can heat up, Maggie. I expect you remember where everything is. And the boy can light the fire."

Sandy had never seen his mother look so worn out and sad. She left the room without a word and Sandy was alone with his grandmother. He stared at the old woman. He couldn't believe she was really as awful as she seemed.

"Well?" she snapped. "What are *you* looking at? I believe in saying what's on my mind. Your mother knows that. Now you do too. Light the fire!"

*I guess she **is** as awful as she seems,* Sandy thought to himself.

He bent down to light the fire. He knew the old lady was watching every move he made. It made him nervous. He even had trouble striking the match, and he could tell she didn't think much of him.

She thinks I can't even light a fire, he thought. *I bet she's just waiting to tell me how useless I am.*

But his grandmother had something else on her mind.

"So," she said suddenly. "You look like your father. I expect you don't want to know that. He wasn't much of a father to you, was he? He vanished before you were born. All the time you were growing up, he wasn't there. I expect you probably hate him."

Sandy didn't answer. He'd felt a lot of things about his father. When he was little he didn't believe his dad was really dead. He kept on hoping that the next man to walk down his road would be *him*, come back again, with an amazing story about where he'd been and why he'd had to leave. Then, after a while, he decided his father must be dead after all. And that made him sad. Sad, but also angry, so angry he'd wake up in the middle of the night, shaking. And then, a few years ago he made himself stop thinking about it any more. And now he *didn't* think about it.

But he was never going to tell this awful old woman any of that! Not that she'd listen anyway.

"*You* think he drowned," she went on. "Or ran away. That will be what your mother told you."

"She says he was lost. That's all," Sandy muttered.

The old woman stared at him. He tried to out-stare her, but it was like out-staring a stone. He looked down at his feet.

Mrs Grey snorted. "No need to be rude," she said in her cold, old voice. "And your mother's right. He *was* lost. Just not in the way you think."

"What do you mean?" said Sandy.

"I mean, there're worse things than drowning," said Mrs Grey. She looked as if she were about to say more when Sandy's mum called from the kitchen.

"Grub's up!"

Mrs Grey's mouth went tight, like a rusty shut letter-box, but Sandy grinned. His mum used to call him for meals like that when he was little and playing at being a cowboy. She was trying to make him feel better. She was trying to fight back!

"Coming!" he called.

"No need to shout," snapped the old woman. "Push me!"

I'd like to push you, he thought to himself, *right off the cliff!* But out loud he just said, "Yes, Mrs Grey."

And he turned the wheel-chair round and headed for the kitchen.

Chapter 2
The Dare

Sandy woke up early the next morning. It was hard to sleep in this house. The bed was lumpy and damp. The endless crashing of the sea had kept him awake for a long time the night before and he was feeling muzzy and unhappy.

He got dressed and went out onto the cliff top – anything to get away from the house from hell! As he stared down, over the cliff, at the sea below, he thought about his father.

Had *he* felt the same way? Had he looked down at the sea and wanted to escape?

Sandy shivered in the cold wind. There was something about the way the waves smashed into the rocks below, again and again. He couldn't look away. The endless moving water seemed to draw him. The crashing sounds that went on and on seemed to call him. If he listened just a little bit longer he was sure he would make out a voice, crying to him, trying to tell him something ...

"SANDY! BE CAREFUL!"

It was his mum. There was panic in her eyes. He saw that he was really close to the edge of the cliff now, and he stepped back quickly.

"Oops. Sorry!" he said to her. "I didn't mean to scare you."

"Just be careful," she said. "It's not safe around here. The cliff edge can crumble or you could get trapped by the sea down at the shore or – "

" – or the sheep could get me!" Sandy said with a grin.

"No, it's the Kelpies that will get you round here," said his mum. She was smiling too, but it was a put-on smile. She didn't look happy. "Do you know about the Kelpies? They're killer horses that come out of the sea and turn into beautiful women or dazzling men and then drown you. Or eat you. Or turn you into their slave."

"OK, Mum," said Sandy. "I think we can safely say you've now gone bonkers."

"24 hours here – that was all it took!" she laughed. "Let's go in – I'm cold!"

As they turned to go back to the house, Sandy pointed to the bay below and asked, "How do you get down there? I thought I might get some photos ..." Then he saw the look on his mum's face. "*Now* what's wrong?" he said.

"Nothing," she spoke too quickly. "It's just ... your father liked to take photos."

"Really? I didn't know that."

She gave a nervous laugh. "Just before he vanished he spent all the money we had on a big, fancy camera. The search party found it, all smashed up. That, and a horse's bridle that had been ripped to shreds."

Weird! thought Sandy. What would his dad be doing with a horse's bridle? Where would he ever get a horse? He wanted to ask more about it, but his mum was still talking.

"I hate this place, Sandy," she said in a low voice. "And it hates me. Even the people hate me – your grandmother for one, and then there was a local girl. Janet MacGann. Everyone thought she and your father would get married some day. Until I came along and stole him!"

"But that was a million years ago!" said Sandy. "No one's going to remember anything from way back then!"

His mum gave him a look. "Just be careful," she said.

There was no school yet, because it was the Easter break. But Sandy knew he'd have to deal with more than just his gruesome grandmother in this new life. There'd be the kids who lived round here too. There'd be a gang. There always was.

Next day, he was coming back from town with some shopping for his mum. As he stepped off the bus, the gang was waiting for him.

Anyone could see who the leader was. Sandy saw a lot of little kids out of the corner of his eye but he knew they weren't important. It was the girl at the front that mattered.

"I'm Caitlin MacGann," she said.

She was as tall as him but so skinny it looked as if her bones were trying to escape. She had black hair as straight as a sheet, and pale grey eyes and white, white skin. And no spots.

What kind of teenager has no spots? he thought to himself. *Maybe she's not really a teenager at all. Maybe she's an alien.*

In movies, aliens mostly wanted to rip your guts out. But maybe this girl was a *friendly* alien. Then he looked into those pale eyes, and saw the look on her face.

Not a friendly alien, he thought with a sigh.

"Ah, jeez, Caitlin, I can't fight *him* – look at the *size* of him!" one of the boys said.

Not for the first time, Sandy was glad he was so big. People thought twice before they tried to push him into fighting. The girl looked at him, as if she hoped he might shrink if she stared hard enough. Then she gave a shrug.

"OK – so he's too big to fight. But then what do we do about him joining the gang?"

Sandy knew he couldn't say, *I don't want to be in your stupid gang, anyway.* He waited. The others looked nervous and waited too.

"What about a test?" Caitlin said at last.

Oh-oh, thought Sandy. "What kind of a test?" he asked with a frown. He knew about tests and dares. They could get nasty.

"Well, let's say we'll give you a choice."

No one said a word. Everyone was looking at her, but Caitlin didn't seem fussed. She took her time.

"Well, let's see … We dare you. How about you steal a hundred cigarettes? Or you wear a sheet and jump out at Daft Old Frank. That weirdo's always saying he sees ghosts. It'd be fun to see what happens if he really *does* see one! Or, I don't know, you could … you could spend tonight in the Bay at the Sea's Back. You can choose one of those."

Sandy heard the other kids whispering, but Caitlin just kept on looking at him. She wanted an answer.

So he gave her one.

"The Bay thing," he said. "But I think all those dares are pretty stupid." His mum had already warned him that some of the bays got cut off when the sea came in. The Bay at the Sea's Back must be one of those. But he wasn't going to give some old man a heart attack to please this Caitlin MacGann, and he wasn't going to get caught shop-lifting, either. A night out would be boring and cold, but it wouldn't get him in trouble.

A no-brainer, really.

So then why was Caitlin looking so smug all of a sudden, and why were the others looking so worried?

"That's not funny, Caitlin," said a small boy. "He doesn't know. You *can't* make him do that. It's not right."

"Make him?" said Caitlin. "I'm not making him do anything."

"I'll do it tonight," said Sandy. He started to walk away, but she called after him, "Don't try to cheat! Take some photos. I'll want proof!"

Sandy didn't turn around. She knew he'd heard.

Chapter 3
Mrs Grey's Pearls

That night, Sandy was on his way to the front door when a voice called him back.

"You. Sandy. Come here." It was his grandmother.

Sandy gave a sigh. *So much for sneaking out*, he thought.

His mum had got the old woman into bed and then said good-night and gone to bed herself. She was worn out. But Mrs Grey was still wide awake and alert as a cat. Sandy gave another sigh and went into her bedroom.

"Young Bill MacIntosh's mother rang me this evening," Mrs Grey began. "Her boy told her about the dare. It was that girl Caitlin MacGann, wasn't it? There's nasty blood in the MacGann family. I should've known she'd find a way to send you to the Bay. Her mother, Janet, was dead set on your father all those years ago, before he met Maggie. I've often asked myself if it was Janet who put that stupid idea in his head."

"What idea?"

Mrs Grey looked at him, her mouth tight and grim.

"The idea of taking a photo of the Kelpies," she said.

Sandy couldn't believe what he'd heard.

"Kelpies? What are you on about?" he burst out. "Kelpies don't exist – they're just fairy tales!"

Mrs Grey snorted. "Your father didn't think so. Why else did he let himself get trapped in the Bay at the Sea's Back, on the night of a full moon, with a storm coming up? He must have thought he'd get a photo of the Kelpies and make a lot of money. The fool thought he'd get away with it! Instead, they got away with him."

What? thought Sandy, and then all at once he understood. His grandmother really thought Kelpies had stolen his father, all those years ago! He remembered what she'd said about his dad vanishing. *There're worse things than drowning,* she'd said. She must be mad!

But she was still talking. "You're as big a fool as your father, so there's no point trying to talk you out of going. Do you have a bridle with you?" And Sandy suddenly remembered what his mum had said – *The search party ... a bridle ripped to shreds.* His brain felt as if it was about to explode. "What do you mean – like, a horse's bridle?" he said.

"What else would I mean?" his grandmother snapped. "Even my son wasn't stupid enough to go looking for Kelpies without taking a bridle. There's some rope in the shed. Or ... there was something my mother told me ... so many years ago, I'd almost forgotten ... Go to my dresser and bring me that box." She pointed a bent finger towards an old wooden box.

Sandy did as he was told.

The old woman unlocked the box, opened it and pulled out a long string of pearls. It

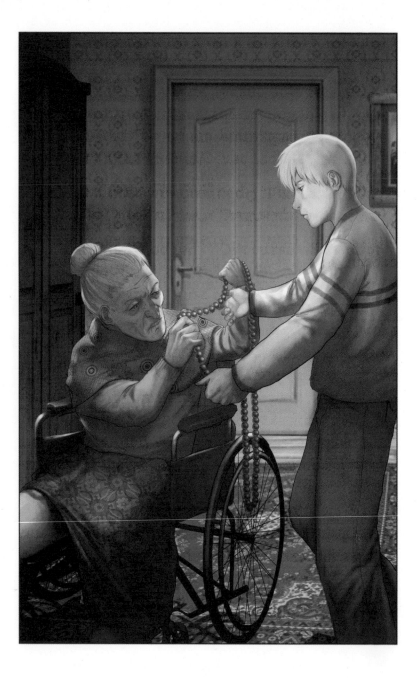

looked as if it was so long, it would go round her neck a few times and still hang down to her waist. She let it slide through her fingers for a moment and then held it out to him.

"What are you giving me *that* for?" said Sandy. "It's a dare, not a fancy dress party."

"It's not *for* you, stupid boy. There's a story about a Kelpie, long ago. And someone caught it – with a bridle made of pearls. I'm not saying it'll work, but I'm giving you the little help I can. Now, you better push off. The sea's coming in fast and you won't be able to get into the Bay. No, wait. There's something in the top drawer. Take that too." And she pointed at the dresser again.

Sandy headed for the door. This was one weird thing too many.

"You're crazy, you know that?" he yelped. "What is it now – a mummy's hand? A cloak of invisibility? What?"

"It's a sweater," said his grandmother. "It'll be cold."

"Oh. Er. Thanks." Sandy fetched the sweater and ran.

Chapter 4
The Bay at the Sea's Back

Sandy shivered. His grandmother was right – it *was* cold! The strip of sand he stood on was getting thinner all the time. He'd made it round the rocky headland to the Bay with only minutes to spare. The sea was coming in so fast, he got soaked to his knees.

Terrific! he groaned. *I get to freeze to death, just so I can join some lame gang. Nice one, Sandy.*

The wind was getting up, whipping the black water into white foam and flying spray. Sandy hugged the sweater tighter round himself and cursed Caitlin and her stupid dare.

He found a rock to shelter behind but even so, the Bay at the Sea's Back was going to be a horrible place to spend the night.

He crouched there and tried to keep warm. He thought about Kelpies. Did his grandmother really believe in them?

And does Caitlin believe in them too? he thought. *Or did she just want me to freeze to death?*

Sandy gave a sigh.

Better take some pictures, he thought. *To prove that I really **was** here, in the middle of the night, like an idiot.*

He got out his camera. The moon was full. Clouds whipped past, but for most of the time, there was enough light.

I'll come back here in the summer, he thought. *I bet I could get some really good pictures then.* He tried some shots of the headland, with the waves bashing up against the rocks at its feet. He checked the viewer. *I'll have to lighten those a lot, but they should still do the job. Good enough for Caitlin MacGann, anyway.*

The noise of the waves pounding onto the rocks was louder now – almost deafening. The wind was howling too, and yet he thought he heard another sound as well. Sandy peered over the top of the rock, trying to work out what this new noise was.

What could be making it?

Something felt very, very wrong. Sandy stepped out from behind the rock ...

... as a herd of horses exploded out of the sea! No normal horse ever looked like these. They were *huge*. Their skin and manes and tails were all bone white – even their eyes were white, like the eyes of dead things. They screamed and kicked and reared up, showing their teeth at each other. But even weirder than that was the fact that everything else around them had suddenly *stopped*.

It was like a freeze frame.

The waves were frozen just before they broke on the beach. The white foam was still and stiff in the air. A second ago, the wind had been whipping Sandy's hair into his eyes. Now there wasn't a breath of air in the Bay. The torn clouds looked as if they had been nailed across the face of the moon. The only sound Sandy could hear was the screaming of the horses – and the thudding of his own heart.

One part of Sandy's brain was yelling *Run!* and another part was shouting *Take a picture!*

I've gone crazy! he thought. His hands were trembling but he lifted his camera and started to click. He took a quick look at the display and groaned. There was nothing showing.

Too dark! he thought and thumbed on the flash.

He clicked again – and all hell broke loose!

The instant the flash went off, all those dead white eyes turned towards him as he stood there in the frozen moonlight. Sandy had never seen such evil glee on an animal's face.

And then, it got worse.

Sandy thought he was going to be sick. The horses turned and twisted and warped as if in terrible pain and all the time they were *changing*. They weren't horses any more – they looked ... human. The beach was suddenly filled with tall, pale people, dressed in what looked like sea-foam. But the evil in their horrible dead white eyes hadn't changed.

KELPIES! Sandy screamed inside his head.

At the front of the crowd was a woman who was taller than the rest. She was more beautiful than any woman Sandy had ever seen – and totally evil. This was the Queen of the Kelpies. Sandy could sense her power. He couldn't look away.

The Kelpies licked their lips. They started to step towards him. There was no escape. He was trapped!

And then something – someone! – who wasn't a Kelpie fell onto the beach in front of Sandy. He wasn't just the shape of a human – he *was* a human. The Kelpies had clothes of beautiful sea-spray foam, but not him. He was dressed in mats of slimy seaweed. He was so thin, you could see his bones. His hair was as white as the Kelpies' but it hung down like dirty string.

He stared at Sandy as if he'd just seen a ghost.

And Sandy felt as if he'd seen one too. He *knew* that face! The man looked just like the photo his mum kept by her bed. He was thinner, and his hair wasn't brown any more. He was much, much older – but he was still the same man.

His father.

And suddenly he knew what his grandmother meant. *There are worse things than drowning*, she'd said. This is what she was talking about. This is what his father's life had been for the last 14 years. Worse than drowning.

"Dad?" he whispered.

The man reached out his hands. But the Queen got there first.

In two strides she reached Sandy and grabbed his chin. She pushed his head back so she could look at him. Her touch made his skin crawl, and her razor-sharp nails left bloody tracks on his skin. She dragged his face back and forth, looking at him from different angles. Then she threw back her own head and neighed out an evil laugh that made hot and cold shivers run down Sandy's spine.

"It's true!" she snarled. "It's written all over his face – he's yours! You never told me you had a son!" And she pushed Sandy away and turned on his father. She hit him hard across the side of the head. Robert Grey landed on the beach with a groan, and curled up, as if expecting a beating. The other Kelpies whistled and squealed. They were looking forward to this, Sandy could tell. But this time, it wasn't going to happen.

He wasn't going to let it happen. That was his dad – and no one beat up on his dad while he was there!

"STOP!" yelled Sandy.

It was only when all the Kelpies' eyes were fixed on him that he knew he didn't have a plan ...

Chapter 5
Sandy Grey's Plan

"Why?" purred the Queen. "Why should I stop?"

The words came out of Sandy's mouth before he even knew he'd thought them. "Because I ... I've got something for you," he stuttered. "I have ... I have magic paintings. Of you. They're ... magic." He groaned inside – did he really think anything so stupid would work? And yet the Queen had stopped hitting his father and was coming slowly towards *him* now.

"Pictures? Show me," she said. There was a weird light in her white eyes.

Slowly Sandy took out his camera. The night was cold but he was sweating, and his hands didn't seem to work any more. It took him forever to get the setting right.

"Well?" The Queen was starting to prowl up and down the beach.

Sandy turned the viewer round to show it to her.

For a long moment she stared down at the tiny blurred picture.

"Is that it?" she said. Her voice dripped scorn.

"Well, um, of course I could print to any size you like. Big would be best, but you might lose a bit of definition … It might be a bit fuzzy." Sandy knew he was talking too much but he couldn't stop. He was shaking all over.

The Queen spat on the beach and turned away.

"I should have known. There's nothing you can give me that I want."

Sandy's heart was beating so hard he could feel his chest move. The Kelpies giggled and yelped.

"Let's eat him now – can we eat him now?" screeched one. "I love it when they're still breathing – the blood's so much, ooo, *redder*."

"Not me, I like them best ever so lightly drowned," yowled another. "Brings out the flavour ..."

I'm going to die, Sandy screamed inside his head. *I'm going to die!*

Then the Queen of the Kelpies had another idea.

"Unless ... yes, there *is* something I can think of ..."

She looked over at Robert, on his knees in the sand, and her dead white eyes gleamed.

Sandy didn't know what she meant, but his father did.

"NO!" he sobbed. "No, Majesty – I beg you!"

She ignored him. "I'm bored with the old human," she said. "He's almost worn out – "

"We could still eat him!" yipped a Kelpie. "He's still mostly fresh!"

The Queen gave a shrug. "If you want. When I've got hold of this new one. Yes, I like this plan. You. Boy. Look at me."

"No – son, don't! Don't look at her!" Robert Grey cried out. "She'll make you her slave ..." A Kelpie fist knocked him to the ground again.

The Queen laughed and bent down until she was looking Sandy right in the eyes. He could feel a horrible pain in his head, as if something was pushing its way into his brain.

"Get off!" He tried to shout but it came out as a whisper. "Leave me alone!"

"Almost there," the Queen whispered. "Just a few more seconds ..."

Sandy felt as if his bones were turning into water. There was nothing he could do. She would control him. There was no escape from those eyes. Not ever ...

"No ... no, please, I ..." whispered Sandy, and Robert cried, "No! No!"

The Queen smiled.

Then his father found his last bit of strength and threw himself at the Queen. He knocked her sideways.

The Kelpie screamed. For that one second, she no longer held Sandy with her eyes.

"Run!" rasped his father – but where could Sandy run? Where could he hide?

And in that moment, Sandy touched the rope of cold smooth pearls which lay forgotten in his pocket.

There wasn't time to think. In one quick movement, he pulled the pearls out and flung them over the terrible creature's head.

The second the pearls touched her skin, the Kelpie Queen opened her mouth to scream again – but no sound came. She clawed at the rope as if it burned her flesh but it was stuck fast. She could not escape. Her face twisted in anger and pain. But still no sound came from her lips.

Sandy backed away.

"What's happening?" he whispered to his father. "Why doesn't she speak?"

"She can't," Robert answered. "She can't speak or leave or do anything. You're in control now. She has to obey you. You've bridled her. Bridled her with pearls. There's no stronger hold you could put on her. How on earth did you know about that?"

Sandy shook his head. "I didn't," he croaked. "Mrs Grey – your mother, I mean – she gave me the pearls. I thought she was crazy." He couldn't understand what his father was saying to him. "You mean, she's our slave? We can make her do things?"

An odd look came over Robert's face. For a moment his eyes went horrible, just like a Kelpie's eyes. Then he gave a long, deep sigh.

"I think there's been enough of that," he said.

Sandy stared at him. "You don't want her to do anything for you? Nothing at all?"

"Well ... maybe just one thing ..." said Robert Grey.

Chapter 6
Robert Grey's Choice

Afterwards, Sandy couldn't exactly remember what happened next. One second they were down by the shore, trapped between the sea and the steep cliffs. The next second, they were on top of the cliff – Sandy, his father, and the silent white horse that was the Kelpie Queen.

Had he really seen Robert whisper in the Queen's ear? Had she changed from a woman back into a horse, there on the beach, and had they really got up onto her back and held tight to her white mane? Had she really leapt up the sheer face of rock to the top with Sandy and Robert on her back? That was impossible. *Nothing* could leap that high. And yet ...

He could see the Grey house in the moonlight, just up the hill. They'd escaped the Bay at the Sea's Back. They were safe!

"What now?" he whispered.

"We let her go," said his father. "You take off the bridle, and we let her go."

"You're sure?" Sandy looked at the thin, pale man standing beside him. What must he have suffered for all those years?

He must really hate her, he thought. *He must be tempted to make her suffer too.*

But mostly Robert just looked tired. As if he wanted it all to be over.

So Sandy reached out his hand and slipped the rope of pearls over the Kelpie's head. For a moment, nothing happened. And then, between one blink and the next, she was gone. Nothing exploded. There were no flashing lights. Nothing dramatic. The Kelpie Queen just wasn't there any more. There was only the empty cliff top ... and his father.

They didn't move. There was an awkward silence.

"So, um, son," said his father. "What's your name?"

"I'm Sandy," said Sandy.

"Sandy." His father seemed to be trying it out. "Nice name ... Do you like it?"

Sandy shrugged. "It's OK."

Silence.

"And you're interested in photography?" said Robert.

"Yeah," said Sandy.

Silence.

"I don't suppose any of the photos of the Kelpies *I* took turned out," said Robert.

"No. Sorry. Mum told me that your camera was smashed up," Sandy said.

Robert gave a sigh. "I thought so."

"You can look at my pictures. If you want to," said Sandy.

That perked Robert up. "That's right – we can sell *your* pictures for a lot of money!"

Sandy shook his head. "I don't think so. No one would believe them. They'd think it was just Photoshop or something like that."

Robert looked puzzled. "Photoshop? What's that?"

And Sandy knew that there was going to be an awful lot to teach this new-found father of his.

"I'll tell you later," he said. "Look, a lot of stuff has changed since you've been, you know, away."

Robert's pale face got even paler.

"Do you mean ... are you trying to tell me ... is this about ..." he stammered and then blurted out, "How's your mother?"

Sandy grinned. "She's fine. Trying not to kill *your* mother! But no, she's not married to anyone else. If that's what you're asking."

Robert threw back his head and neighed in joy.

"Dad," said Sandy. He put a hand on his father's arm. "You really are going to have to stop doing that."

"Oops," said Robert Grey.

And with that, they walked up the hill to home.

BATTLE CARDS

Joan Lennon

Author

Favourite hero:
Aragorn from *The Lord of the Rings*.
Well, let's be honest – it's really Viggo
Mortensen who acts as Aragorn in the
film!

Favourite monster:
The Uraki Chief in *The Lord of the Rings*
when somebody put a pink flower in his
hair. (Also because the Uraki have
great music.)

Your weapon of choice:
A flying horse. Partly so I can get
away, and partly so that my horse
can poo on my enemies' heads.

Favourite fight scene:
Gandalf v. the Balrog.

RELOADED

Daniel Atanasov

Illustrator

Favourite hero:
I like huge characters like Potemkin (Guilty Gear Arcade Game).

Favourite monster:
Tessai, one of the five devils who destroyed the Koga ninja clan (Ninja scroll).

Your weapon of choice:
Something heavy like a two handed sword or a war hammer. There are too many to choose only one!

Special secret power:
My venom.

Goodie or baddie:
I've always wanted to be the good guy. But I never am :(

RELOADED

Barrington Stoke would like to thank all its readers for commenting on the manuscript before publication and in particular:

Ikram Abdi
Abdullah Ahmed
Dana Abdullah
William Allardyce
Chris Baillie
Valentina Bogujevci
Toni Clifford
Josh Fletcher
Cammy Galloway
Ryan Garcia
Gurjinder Grewal
Leon Lloyd Hall
Thomas Harrison
Ayesha Iqbal

Amaan Khan
Mikey Kingston
Ivana Koralek
Corey Mayes
Aoife McCafferty
Ruta Michael
Shilan Mirza
Stefano Navarra
Noshin
Reggie Swali
Shona Thomson
C. Williams
Jordan Wilson
Mrs Woodward

Become a Consultant!

Would you like to be a consultant? Ask your parent, carer or teacher to contact us at the email address below – we'd love to hear from them! They can also find out more by visiting our website.

schools@barringtonstoke.co.uk
www.barringtonstoke.co.uk

THE LAMBTON CURSE

BY
MALACHY DOYLE

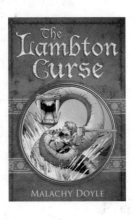

A terrible monster is on the loose. An evil worm.
It sucks its victims dry, leaving nothing but an
empty bag of skin. It eats everything it sees.
And it's all Young Lambton's fault. He let the
monster out. He ran away. Now he's come back to
kill it … or die trying.

You can order *The Lambton Curse* directly from
www.barringtonstoke.co.uk

THE GENIE OF TIMBUKTU

BY
GILL HARVEY

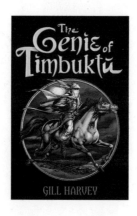

He wears all white and rides a white horse.
All you can see is his eyes of fire – eyes that can
burn your soul.
He is the Genie of Timbuktu. The most powerful
genie there is.
But does he have the power to save Abdul's life?